SLAM

Go to Hawaii

Written by Chris Sawyer
Illustrated by Dennis Hockerman

HOOKED ON
PHONICS™

SLAM & DUNK™

Go to Hawaii

Contents

Special Words

Special words help make this story fun.
Your child may need help reading them.

Hawaii

parrot

turtle

volcano

wave

whale

1. What Can We Do?

It's summer, it's hot, and it's Monday.

"What do you want to do?" asks Slam.

"I do not know," says Dunk. "It's too hot for a game of basketball."

"Do you want to play checkers?" asks Slam.

"No," says Dunk. "We did that for the last six days. Why not go swimming?"

That's when Slam and Dunk go down to the kitchen. Grandpa is there. He has a big grin. He's got something in his hands, but Slam and Dunk cannot see what it is.

"Do not look," says Grandpa. "See if you can think of what I have in my hands."

"A sandwich!" says Slam.
"A cactus!" says Dunk.

"No," says Grandpa. "Look! This is what we will do for fun today!"

"Go fishing!" yell Slam and Dunk. "What a good idea!"

So, Slam and Dunk and Grandpa
go down to the river. They go out
onto the dock. They cast, and
PLUNK! Into the water goes the
fishing fly.

They sit. They sit a bit longer. Then Slam asks, "How long does it take to catch a fish?"

"Sometimes it can take a very long time," says Grandpa. "You cannot rush the fish, you know."

"I want to catch a really big fish," says Dunk. "Little fish are no fun."

"I did not know that," says Grandpa with a grin. "Sometimes, it's the big fish that are not that much fun."

That's when Dunk gets a big tug on his fishing rod. The tug is so big, Dunk thinks he will get yanked off the dock.

"What do I do now?" he yells.

"Hang on!" yells Grandpa. "Do not let go! Whatever you do, do not let that big fish yank you into the water!"

That's when Dunk begins to skid.

Slam grabs onto Dunk so he will not skid right off the dock.

"Help!" yells Slam.

"Oh no!" yells Dunk, as his hat lands in the water.

"I think you got your wish!"
yells Grandpa.

"I did not wish to get yanked
into the water!" says Dunk.

"But you did wish for a big fish,"
says Grandpa, "and this must be
a very big fish!"

2. That's a Big Fish!

All of a sudden, the rod snaps. The
tugging stops. Slam and Dunk and
Grandpa look. There in the water
is a big, black bump. The bump is
looking right at them!

It's a whale!

"Does this belong to you?" asks the whale. He has Dunk's hat. He puts it on the dock right next to Slam and Dunk.

"Thank you!" says Dunk.

"I did not know that whales swim in this river," says Grandpa.

"We do not," says the whale. "I was on a little trip, but now I am going back home."

"Where is that?" asks Slam.

"Hawaii," says the whale. "Do you want to come with me?"

"Can we, please?" Slam and Dunk ask Grandpa.

"It's a long trip," says Grandpa. "Can you get them back by six?"

"Yes," says the whale. "I am a very fast swimmer."

"OK," says Grandpa. "Have fun!"

Slam and Dunk hop onto the
whale's back. The whale takes off.
He swims in the water so fast that
Dunk has to hang onto his hat.

"How long will it take us to get
to Hawaii?" asks Slam.

"Look over there!" says the whale. "That's Hawaii!"

"That was very quick," says Dunk.

"I said I was fast!" says the whale.

Slam and Dunk look down. They see lots of fish. There are red fish and pink fish swimming past big rocks. There are puffer fish and trigger fish. There are lots of shellfish on the bottom.

Just then, there is a splash right next to them.

It's a turtle!

"I am so glad you are back!" says the turtle. "You must help!"

"What's the matter?" asks the whale.

"We think there will be a problem with the volcano!"

"How do you know?" ask Slam
and Dunk.

"The gulls said so," says the turtle.

"Does that mean the volcano
will blast?" asks the whale.

"We do not know," says the turtle.

3. Let's Catch a Wave

That's when they see some gulls.
"Will the volcano blast?" asks
the turtle.
"We do not know," say the gulls.
"But that is what the parrots said."

"We must check with the parrots," says the turtle.

"But we must get all of the little fish to a good spot now. If the water gets too hot, it will be bad for them," says the whale.

"We can help," says Slam.

"What can we do?" asks Dunk.

"Go with the billfish," says the whale. "I will take all of the little fish past the reef and tell the moms and dads."

"Do you think the volcano will blast?" asks Dunk.

"I do not know," says the billfish. "You see, I cannot go up on land to check."

"We can do that!" says Slam.

"But how do we get to land from here?" asks Dunk.

"Just do what I tell you to do," says the billfish.

Just then, a big wave comes.

"Swim as fast as you can to catch the wave," says the billfish. "Then 'hang ten' until you get to land!"

Slam and Dunk swim until they catch the wave. Then they ride on the wave right up to a good spot on the sand.

From there they can see the volcano.

"We forgot to ask what the volcano does when it blasts," says Dunk.

"Let's go up there and see if we run into a parrot who can tell us," says Slam.

Slam and Dunk go up into the forest. There are lots of big red flowers. They can't see well in the mist. But they do see a flock of parrots.

"Stop!" they yell. "Please tell us if the volcano will blast."

"We do not know," say the parrots. "That is what the pigs said."

4. On the Volcano

"Tell us where the pigs are so we can ask them," says Dunk.

"Go up to the top of the forest, and then take the path to the left," says a parrot. "Then you will be on the volcano. That is where the pigs like to play."

Slam and Dunk go past more flowers. A big butterfly tells them where the path is. They go left on the path until the mist ends.

A bunch of pigs are playing in the grass.

"Can you please tell us if the volcano will blast?" ask Slam and Dunk.

"We do not think so," say the pigs. "Why do you ask?"

"Well, the turtle said the gulls said so," says Slam.

"The gulls said the parrots said so," says Dunk.

"The parrots said you pigs said so," says Slam.

"We did not say that," say the pigs.

"Who did?" asks Dunk.

"They must have gotten mixed up," says a pig. "We said that playing on this volcano is a blast!"

"I get it," says Dunk. "That's when the parrots got mixed up. They think you said, 'The volcano will blast!'"

"That's right!" say the pigs. "We play here all of the time, so they think we know what the volcano will do."

"They are right," says a pig. "But the volcano will not blast."

"We have to tell the fish now," says Slam. "They are very upset."

"I know what to do," says Dunk. "A parrot can fly down and tell them for us. They are faster than we are."

Just then, a flock of parrots is flying by. Slam and Dunk get them to stop.

The pigs say, "Tell the whale, the turtle, and the billfish that the volcano will not blast."

"No problem," say the parrots, and off they fly.

"Thank you," say the pigs. "We did not want to upset the fish. We did not know they would think that."

"Well," say Slam and Dunk, "the little fish will be OK now."

5. The Best Game Ever

"We have to go back soon," says
Slam.

"Oh no!" say the pigs. "Can't you
play a game with us?"

"What game do you want to
play?" ask Slam and Dunk.

"We think the best game is basketball," say the pigs. "But we will play whatever game you want to play."

"Basketball!" say Slam and Dunk. "That is the best game ever!"

"We think so, too," say the pigs.
"This is where we play, and this
is the basket."

The pigs grab a ball and say,
"Let's go!"

A pig tosses up the ball, and—BAM!—into the basket it goes!

"Good shot," says Slam. "This will be a fun game!"

He tosses the ball up and WAM! "It's in!" yell the pigs.

Dunk runs up and slams a shot. But the ball hits the rim. Slam grabs the ball next. He runs up to make a shot, but it is a miss.

The pig runs and gets the ball
from Dunk. He slams a shot.
BAM! It's in the basket!
"Good shot!" yells Slam.

"That's 2 for you and 2 for us!"
yells Dunk. "But I bet we will win!"

Slam and Dunk and the pigs play
and play. It is now 10 for Slam and
Dunk and 10 for the pigs.

Dunk wants to run and get the ball to Slam, but a pig runs up and blocks him. The pig goes to grab the ball from Dunk. He jumps up, but Slam runs over to him.

"Pass the ball to me!" yells Slam.
Dunk tosses the ball. Slam grabs
the ball. He jumps up. He jams it
into the basket.

WAM!

"It's in!" yells Dunk.

"The game is over!" yells Slam.

"You win," yell the pigs. "But we had a very good game!"

"Thank you for letting us play," say Slam and Dunk. "But now we need to get back."

"We are glad you had such a good time," say the pigs, "but how come you have to go?"

"Grandpa said we must be back by six," say Slam and Dunk.

The pigs all say good-bye as Slam and Dunk run down into the forest.

They get back to the sand and see the whale.

"Swim out and jump on my back," he says. "We need to get going!"

"Thank you so much for taking
us to Hawaii," say Slam and Dunk.
"Can we come back and see you?"

"Please do," says the whale. "I
will stop and check on you now
and then. You can come back with
me whenever you like."

Grandpa is on the dock when Slam and Dunk get back.

"Did you have a good time?" he asks.

"Yes, we did," says Slam.

"We played basketball, and we got to see a volcano," says Dunk.

"That's very good," says Grandpa. "And you got a big fish for a pal, too."